PUFFIN BOOKS

STORM GHOST

Louise Cooper was born in Hertfordshire in 1952. She hated school so much – spending most lessons clandestinely writing stories – that she persuaded her parents to let her abandon her education at the age of fifteen, and has never regretted it. Her first novel was published when she was twenty. Moving to London in 1975, she worked in publishing before becoming a full-time writer in 1977. Since then she has published more than twenty fantasy novels, in both the adult and children's fields, and has ideas for many more to come. She also writes occasional short stories, and poetry for her own pleasure.

Louise Cooper lives in an area sandwiched between the Cotswolds and the Malverns and gains a great deal of inspiration from the scenery. She is also potty about cats and steam trains!

Some other books by Louise Cooper

HEART OF DUST
HEART OF FIRE
HEART OF GLASS
HEART OF ICE
HEART OF STONE

SURFERS

Storm
Ghost

Louise Cooper

Illustrated by
David Frankland

PUFFIN BOOKS

For Cas,
who didn't laugh (too much!)
at a landlubber's ignorance,
and turned the leaky boat into
something seaworthy

PUFFIN BOOKS

Published by the Penguin Group
Penguin Books Ltd, 27 Wrights Lane, London W8 5TZ, England
Penguin Putnam Inc., 375 Hudson Street, New York, New York 10014, USA
Penguin Books Australia Ltd, Ringwood, Victoria, Australia
Penguin Books Canada Ltd, 10 Alcorn Avenue, Toronto, Ontario, Canada M4V 3B2
Penguin Books (NZ) Ltd, 182–190 Wairau Road, Auckland 10, New Zealand

Penguin Books Ltd, Registered Offices: Harmondsworth, Middlesex, England

First published 1998
5 7 9 10 8 6 4

Text copyright © Louise Cooper, 1998
Illustrations copyright © David Frankland, 1998
All rights reserved

The moral right of the author and illustrator has been asserted

Typeset in Bembo

Made and printed in England by Clays Ltd, St Ives plc

British Library Cataloguing in Publication Data
A CIP catalogue record for this book is available from the British Library

ISBN 0–140–38636–X

Contents

1 Bad Weather 1

2 Missing! 16

3 Out of the Past 31

4 Cry for Help 42

5 Riding the Storm 56

6 Breakdown 71

7 Man Overboard! 82

8 Cold Light of Dawn 92

9 Secrets 104

10 Headline News 117

Chapter One
Bad Weather

THE WEATHER WAS keeping Mark awake.
Storm clouds had started to gather over the sea that morning and now, at nearly midnight, the wind was rampaging wildly. It howled through the village, battering against the eaves and rattling his window like something

monstrous trying to burst in. Mark's bedroom overlooked Polkerran harbour and, as well as the racket of the wind, he could hear the sea roaring. It sounded huge and sinister and dangerous.

So much for Cornish holidays, Mark thought sourly. He had been enjoying his stay here, at the One and All pub. His Uncle Chris, Mum's brother, was the landlord and this was Mark's first visit on his own. Until now, it had been great. But *this* . . .

He pulled the duvet over his head, trying to blot the noise out. Then suddenly, from somewhere nearby, came a muffled but urgent bleeping noise.

Blinking, Mark sat up. He was just

starting to ask himself where the bleeping had come from, or if he'd imagined it, when without any warning a colossal *BANG!* echoed through the village.

"*What the —*" Mark shot out of bed, thinking horribly of bombs, and rushed to the window. The moon showed through piling, racing clouds and the sea was heaving and surging, spray pounding up over the harbour wall. Lights were coming on all over Polkerran and seconds later a silhouetted figure, then another and another, went running full-tilt along the street. What was going *on*?

Footsteps thudded outside his door and his cousin Ritchie Paynter burst in, pulling on a sweater as he ran.

"Ritchie!" Mark blurted in alarm. "What was that noise? What's going on?"

"Lifeboat's been called out!" Ritchie said breathlessly, flailing his arms into his sleeves. "Roy's bleeper went just now − you know he's in the crew − then they let off the maroon in case anyone hasn't got the message! That's what the huge bang was. You coming?"

"Coming where?"

"Lifeboat house, where else?"

Mark didn't need any urging. He grabbed his clothes and in seconds both boys were racing downstairs. They were in time to see Roy, Ritchie's elder brother, dashing out of the front door, then Mark's uncle appeared, pulling on his oilskins.

"Dad!" Ritchie called. "Can we come with you?"

Mr Paynter nodded. "All right. But be quick – and when we get there, keep out of everyone's way!"

Within another minute, the three of them piled out into the night. The wind hit Mark like a sledgehammer and nearly knocked him off his feet. Uncle Chris grabbed him, yelled something that Mark couldn't hear above the racket of wind and sea, then, heads down, butting into the gale, they set off.

The stumbling run along the harbour front was like a wild, crazy dream. There was a huge roaring in Mark's ears and seething darkness all around him. The gale made him stagger and veer from side to side. Waves were surging furiously against the harbour wall, hitting it with a thundering *boom!* that shook the ground under his feet. The wind hurled great cascades of spray over the road; it felt like hailstones hitting him and Mark turned his head aside, gasping for breath in the onslaught.

The lifeboat house was ahead — a black silhouette crouching on the hard. They stumbled inside to a world of bright light and hectic activity: the crew pulling on their gear, people shouting instructions, radio equipment crackling. Dominating it all was the sleek shape of the lifeboat itself.

She was a Waveney class, Mark had learned, about fourteen metres long and designed in America in the 1960s. She was due to be replaced fairly soon and Uncle Chris had said that the crew would be sad to see her go. Standing high on her ramp, she looked big and powerful and proud. But as he blinked at her through stinging eyes, Mark thought of what it must be like to be out on the open sea on a night like this. Unlike his cousins, he was a city boy and the idea terrified the life out of him. Even in that boat, he'd be just too plain scared.

Roy was with the red-haired coxswain by the lifeboat. The cox looked angry and in a lull in the hubbub Mark heard him say, "All right, all right – we've got two men down with flu and another one on holiday, so you'll have to come with us. But that doesn't mean we've got to like it!"

Some of the other crewmen overheard and shot Roy filthy looks, but Roy only shrugged and scowled back. Mark nudged Ritchie. "What's up with them?"

"Nothing," Ritchie replied sharply. There was a frown on his face and Mark knew he was lying. Something *was* up; something between Roy and the rest of the crew. But he had no chance to ask again. The crew had scrambled on board and the boathouse doors were opening. As the scream and roar of the night came surging at them again, someone yelled, "Right – let's get her away!"

Mark felt a lurching thrill in his

stomach as he watched the lifeboat being winched towards the slipway. Forward she went, slowly but surely, nosing out through the doors and into the storming night. She reached the top of the slope and poised there. Then, with a chatter and a snarl, her engines started. Her lights came on, stabbing into the dark, and she tilted on to the slipway and started to gather speed.

"Come on!" Ritchie yelled over the racket. "Let's watch her go!"

They piled outside as the boat made a final rush down the slipway. She hit the water with a shuddering impact and Mark recoiled as twin fountains of white spray, like gleaming knives, shattered up and out from her bow. The engine's throttle opened with a roar that echoed over the noise of wind and sea — then, like an arrow, the lifeboat powered away.

Huddled and buffeted against the wall, Mark watched through screwed-up eyes as the boat headed towards the green and red lights at the harbour entrance. Beyond was the wild, open sea. He thought of shipwreck stories and turned to Ritchie, shouting to make himself heard. "What sort of rescue is it?"

Ritchie shook his head. "They don't know yet. Coastguard got a distress call from some boat — they know she's adrift and where she is, but that's all. Could be a cargo ship or just some prat in a yacht who can't navigate! Could be an oil tanker on fire, for all we know!"

Mark shuddered. "Think of trying to get near something like that!"

"If that's what it is, they'll do it. Got to, haven't they?"

"Doesn't it scare you?" Mark knew that Ritchie wanted to join the lifeboat crew as soon as he was old enough. It was a long tradition in the Cornish side of the family, though it was all very new to Mark. But what his cousins didn't know about boats and the sea wasn't worth knowing and Uncle Chris had been in the crew too, until a knee injury playing football had made him unfit.

Ritchie only shrugged and said, "Course it scares me – I'd be an idiot if it didn't! I've seen how these guys look when they come back from a rescue.

They're half dead with exhaustion sometimes. But you expect that. It's all part of the excitement."

"Well, I'll do without that sort of excitement, thanks!"

A voice called out of the dark, "You two ready?" Uncle Chris appeared. "Time we were getting back," he told them, "or Mum'll have my guts for garters!"

Mark peered into the howling dark, but he couldn't see the lifeboat now. Then, as they all braced themselves to face the wind and spray again, Ritchie said, "Dad – Roy'll be OK, won't he? With the others, I mean, after what he –"

"Shut up, Ritch," Uncle Chris interrupted. His voice was tense.

"But —"

"I said, shut up! Roy's fine. Forget it, all right?"

Ritchie looked miserable. "All right."

Mark remembered what had happened earlier, and his feeling that something was wrong between Roy and the rest of the crew. Looking at his uncle's face, then at Ritchie's, he thought better of asking any questions. But he was suddenly very, very curious.

After the excitement of the launch, Mark thought that nothing on earth could make him sleep. But to his surprise, he was out like a light almost as soon as his head touched the pillow.

It was morning when he woke and dreary grey daylight was coming in through the window. The wind had dropped but the sea beyond the harbour was a heaving, grey-and-white turmoil. Angry clouds were piling up over the sea again and it looked as if there was more bad weather to come.

From his window Mark saw that there were quite a lot of people on the quay. He looked for the lifeboat but couldn't see her or any of the crew. Either they weren't back yet or the boat was out of sight further along the harbour. Yawning, Mark pulled his clothes on and went downstairs.

There was no smell of breakfast. In fact the house seemed unnaturally quiet and, as he reached the bottom of the stairs, Mark started to feel uneasy. Where *was* everyone? Then Ritchie appeared.

"Ritchie, where's —?" Mark started to say, but stopped when he saw Ritchie's white face. His stomach churned uneasily. "What's wrong? What's happened?"

Ritchie stared at him. "It's the lifeboat," he said in a flat, dead voice. "They lost radio contact with her an hour after she went out. She hasn't come back, Mark. She's disappeared."

Chapter Two
Missing!

THE HELICOPTER SWEPT over the village
with a *thub-thub-thub* of rotor blades.
Mark, standing with Ritchie on the quay,
craned his head to watch as it flew above
the harbour and away like a huge, dark
bird towards the cliffs and the open sea.

Ritchie's fists were clenched at his

sides. "They've got to find her," he said starkly. "They've *got* to!"

Mark crossed his fingers as he gazed at the now tiny helicopter. Another crew from the air-sea rescue service was already out there and two lifeboats and the Navy had joined the search. But as yet they had found no trace whatever of the Polkerran boat.

It was raining now and Mark asked uneasily, "What happens if the weather gets worse?"

"Depends," Ritchie said. "If it's just rain, the 'copters can keep flying. But if the gale comes back . . ." He shrugged, trying to appear calm, though Mark knew he was anything but. Then suddenly he added, "You know it was a false alarm, don't you?"

"What?"

"The call-out last night. I heard one of the coastguards say. Three lifeboats went out, including ours, but none of them found any ship in trouble."

"Did the others see your – our – lifeboat?" Mark asked.

"No. Not a sign."

A painful silence fell between the boys. Mark looked along the harbour wall where local people were standing about in small groups. The rain was getting heavier, but no one cared or even noticed. They just stared, grim-faced, out to sea. Nearly everyone in the village was related to at least one of the lifeboat crewmen. What was a soaking, compared with something that threatened to become a personal tragedy for them all?

There was a thought nagging at Mark's mind. He wanted to say it aloud to Ritchie, but every time he tried, his courage failed him. The trouble was, it had a connection with Roy and under the circumstances Mark didn't like to bring the subject of Roy up.

Suddenly, Ritchie said, "What's the point standing around here getting wet? We can't do anything and we can't see anything. I'm going home."

He turned, shoving his hands into his jacket pockets, and slouched away towards the One and All. Mark hesitated a moment, then went after him. He caught up near the door. Two old men were coming towards them and as they passed, one said kindly, "Sorry about your brother, Ritchie-boy."

Ritchie nodded glum thanks, and the other old man grunted, "That Roy . . . gurt fool should have known better'n to do what he did."

The first man turned angrily on him. "Hold your clack, Bill!" Then to Ritchie: "Don't take any notice of 'n, Ritch. They'll come home safe, never you fear!"

The men walked on. For a couple of seconds Ritchie stared after them — then he yanked the door open and ran indoors. Seeing the look on his face, Mark knew he couldn't keep quiet any longer and as soon as the door was shut behind them he said, "What did he mean, Roy should have known better?"

Ritchie didn't answer the question. Instead he went into the bar, saying,

"Mum and Dad have got to open the pub in an hour. I promised I'd get things ready before they come back."

Ritchie's parents were at the lifeboat house, hoping against hope for news. Mark followed Ritchie into the bar and watched as he started setting out stools and mats. "Ritch —" he said.

"Look, Mark," Ritchie interrupted aggressively, "Bill didn't mean anything, all right? He's just a stupid old man."

"Don't give me that," Mark persisted. "Something was wrong last night, wasn't it? Between Roy and the rest of the crew — I saw what happened at the lifeboat house. Come on, Ritch, tell me!"

"No," Ritchie said. "You'll only laugh."

Mark felt insulted. "I'm not going to

laugh at anything while the lifeboat's missing!" he retorted angrily.

"OK, OK. Sorry."

"Well then?"

There was a pause. Then, "It was the song Roy sang."

"What song?" Mark was baffled.

Ritchie sighed and sat down. "Some of the regulars were having a sing-song in here last night," he said. "I could hear them from upstairs. Roy was there too. They asked him to sing something, then this argument started."

"Because of what he sang?"

Ritchie nodded. "It was Trevorgie's song. And no one's supposed to sing that, not ever. The old guys . . . well, they say it's cursed."

Mark stared at him. "It's *what*? Oh,

come on! No one believes things like that!"

"They do round here. You saw for yourself." Suddenly Ritchie got up and walked across the room. "All right; if you really want to know, I'll tell you. Come over here."

He was standing by some old photos that hung on the wall and when Mark joined him he stabbed a finger at one of the pictures. "See that? That's the crew of the *Charlotte Henty*. She was the Polkerran lifeboat in 1925."

The photo showed a group of men in oilskins, standing stiffly in front of an old-fashioned boat. The man in the centre of the group had a heavy black beard, and Mark said, "That's our great-granddad, isn't it? The one who was drowned?"

Over seventy years ago, great-granddad Paynter had been coxswain of the *Charlotte Henty* . . . until tragedy struck and the Polkerran lifeboat had been lost with nearly all her crew. Mark's mum had once told him about that long-ago disaster, but he only remembered the story vaguely. Ritchie, though, didn't seem to want to talk about it; in fact it was hardly ever mentioned by anyone in Polkerran. All Mark knew was that the *Charlotte Henty* had been called out one storm-racked night and had never returned.

Now though, Ritchie said, "Yeah, that's him." He pointed at another figure in the photo. "And that's Joe Trevorgie. He was in the crew too."

Mark stared at Trevorgie. There was

something peculiar about him, he thought; and then he realized what it was. Though his face was young, his hair looked white. Must've been very blond, Mark told himself. Round here, that was unusual.

"Trevorgie wrote a song about the boat," Ritchie said. "The night after he first sang it, the disaster happened."

"So what?" Mark was baffled. "I mean, not so what about the disaster, of course, but you can't blame it on a song!"

"Maybe not." Ritchie sounded bitter. "But you can blame Trevorgie. It was his fault that the lifeboat was lost."

Mark stared. "Why? What did he do?"

Rain hammered suddenly against the

window and with it came a noise like some huge animal howling. The wind was rising again and when Mark looked uneasily out at the harbour, he saw that the sky was turning blue-black. Another gale was coming. He thought of Roy. Of the lifeboat. And of the doomed crew of seventy years ago . . .

"Joe Trevorgie", Ritchie said, quietly and in a tone that made Mark shiver, "was a coward. Because of his cowardice he went crazy – and he killed great-granddad and all the others."

"But . . . *how*?"

The empty room was horribly gloomy now. Shadows shifted in the corners, as if ghosts were stirring and closing in. Ritchie stared at the old photo. And at last Mark heard the story of the tragedy.

On that fateful night, the *Charlotte Henty* had been called out in storm-force winds to a drifting cargo ship. Joe Trevorgie was in the crew and, as they pitched through mountainous seas against a battering gale, he lost his nerve and started to panic.

"He started yelling that something terrible was going to happen," Ritchie said. "Great-granddad tried to calm him down, but he just went on and on. He wanted to turn back and when the others wouldn't, he screamed that he'd curse them all. He went completely berserk. And that was when the fight started . . ."

The lifeboat was approaching the

helpless cargo ship which was drifting dangerously near rocks. As the crew struggled desperately to overpower Joe Trevorgie, one man fell overboard. They tried to reach him and pick him up, but the lifeboat turned broadside to the waves – and the ship they had gone to help swamped them as she wallowed helplessly towards the rocks.

"The *Charlotte Henty* capsized and the drifting ship was wrecked," Ritchie told Mark sombrely. "Another lifeboat pulled five men out of the sea alive. But the rest all died."

"Including Trevorgie?"

Ritchie nodded. Outside, the wind howled dismally again. "People round here reckoned Trevorgie really *did* put a curse on the crew when they wouldn't do what he wanted. Ever since then, they've believed his song's cursed too and if anyone sings it, it'll bring bad luck."

There was a long pause while Mark stared at the photo of the dead crew. Then Ritchie spoke again.

"I know what you're thinking. It's just a load of stupid superstition."

A weird, cold shiver went through Mark, as if someone had pressed an icicle against his spine. "Course it is," he said, trying to convince himself. "Things like that don't *happen*, Ritch."

"No, sure," Ritchie replied. "But Roy sang that song last night. And now the lifeboat's disappeared." Suddenly he swung to face Mark, and in the gloom of the gathering storm his face looked haggard. "You can call that a coincidence if you want to, Mark. But I don't!"

Chapter Three
Out of the Past

THE DAY WENT by like a waking nightmare, with still no news of the lifeboat.

The whole village was gripped by a tension that strained nerves almost to breaking point. Ritchie's parents tried to behave as if everything was normal, but their efforts were a fragile mask.

Ritchie's mum swung between bouts of tearfulness and filthy temper, often yelling at his dad who couldn't seem to keep still for a moment.

Each time the phone rang, everyone's stomach turned over with a mixture of fear and hope and there was a scrambling rush to answer. But it was always a false alarm.

By the time night fell, the wind had risen to a gale again. Rain squalls swept through the village and the noise of the wild sea was a ceaseless, booming thunder. The search had been called off for the night and the latest message from the coastguards said that there was still not even the smallest clue to the lifeboat's fate.

The One and All was nearly empty

but for a few old regulars who sat in corners nursing their glasses of beer. No one wanted to talk. For as time went by, they were facing the grim probability that the Polkerran lifeboat was lost with all hands.

The Paynters and Mark tried to eat a meal of sorts, but no one could face more than a few mouthfuls. Immediately afterwards, Ritchie was sick – strain, his mum said, and not surprising; she was as bad, look at her, shaking like a leaf. She and Ritchie both went to bed and a few minutes later Mark too went up to his room.

He flopped down on the bed, switched his radio on and listened through crackling interference to a local station. The lifeboat's disappearance was the main news story. "With heavy seas off the south Cornish coast and winds gusting at up to sixty miles an hour, hope is beginning to fade for the boat and her crew," the newsreader announced sombrely. "The search will resume at dawn, but a spokesman for the coastguard service said tonight that the worsening weather makes it —"

Mark switched off, not wanting to feel any more miserable than he did already. There was a dull, sick ache inside him. He wished he could throw up like Ritchie, but he couldn't. It probably wouldn't have helped anyway. He simply couldn't stop thinking about the lifeboat.

And about Joe Trevorgie.

It was stupid of course. There couldn't possibly be any connection. Despite what Ritchie had said, it *was* just a hideous coincidence. Yet Mark couldn't shake off a spooky feeling. Roy sang Trevorgie's song and that very same night the lifeboat vanished. *Could* there be such things as curses, and could they come back to life?

"Oh, shut up!" Mark suddenly thumped his pillow, furious with himself. He was getting as bad as some of the locals like that old man, Bill, who had muttered about Roy. Forget Trevorgie, he told himself. It's rubbish. Find something else to think about. Something that makes *sense*.

He rolled over and switched the radio on once more. The station was playing music now and Mark shut his eyes. He didn't want to sleep. He'd just listen for a while . . .

When he opened his eyes again, his watch read two a.m.

Blinking, Mark sat up. How the heck did *that* happen? He had only meant to lie down for a few minutes! Now here he was, still fully dressed and freezing cold because he hadn't had the duvet over him. It must have been the cold that woke him up.

Or was it?

The radio was still on but the battery was going flat and the sound was just a vague burble. Mark turned it off and listened to the sounds of the weather outside. Funny how he had got used to the noise of the storm; the wind and the sea were still roaring but he hardly noticed them now. It was as if he had been hearing them for ever. Yet there was something else. Something nagging at him and giving him a weird feeling in the pit of his stomach . . .

Telling himself it was just nerves, he went to the bathroom. He thought the feeling would go, but it didn't. In fact, it was getting stronger and when he returned to his room, he had a powerful urge to look outside. Unable to fight it, he pulled the curtains back and peered through the window.

The village looked lifeless. Its streets were empty and its houses were black silhouettes with no lights showing anywhere. But there was enough of a storm-glow in the sky to show the harbour. The sea was a mass of churning waves, their white tops shining and eerie. It looked lethal and Mark shivered as he realized that it must be ten times worse out beyond the harbour's shelter.

Impossible to think of anyone surviving in that . . .

Then, as he was about to close the curtains and go back to bed, he saw a light beyond the harbour entrance.

His eyes widened and he peered harder. The light had vanished now. Had he imagined it? No – there it was again! Spray and rain had smeared the window but there couldn't be any mistake. A light, lurching and bobbing on the sea, coming round the point and heading slowly but surely towards the harbour. It was a boat. It *had* to be!

Mark's heart started to pound with excitement. Was it the lifeboat? He had to wake everyone, tell them! He started to rush for the door – then stopped as an awful thought hit him. What if he was wrong and it wasn't the lifeboat? He couldn't raise Uncle Chris and Aunt Jen's hopes, only to see them dashed. He had to make sure.

He hesitated a bare moment, then ran along the passage to Ritchie's room.

"Ritchie!" He shook his cousin's shoulder furiously. "Ritchie, wake up!"

Ritchie writhed under his duvet. "Nuh . . . Goway . . ."

"Wake *up*! There's a boat coming in to the harbour!"

That got through to Ritchie and suddenly he was wide awake. They both dived for the window. "Is it the lifeboat?" Mark asked urgently. "*Is* it?"

"I – I don't know. Can't see clearly enough." Ritchie was shaking, and suddenly he flung the window open. The wind came slamming in, hurling spray in their faces. Mark flinched back, but Ritchie leaned out to see more clearly.

"There's something weird about that light," he shouted above the gale. "It *is* a boat, but –" The words cut off. Then Mark jumped in shock as Ritchie's hand clamped on his arm.

"Mark! Oh my God, look – *look*!"

Mark jostled to the window beside him and looked.

The boat was in the harbour now and they could see her clearly. She was a lifeboat – but not the one they knew. There was no streamlined hull, no high cockpit, no radio aerials. This was an old-fashioned, wooden boat. A sailing boat. And the light that shone from her was not a navigation light, but a pale and ghastly aura that burned like cold fire.

Riding on the sea, cresting the churning waves with a terrible, steady relentlessness, a ghost was sailing out of the past towards them.

Chapter Four
Cry for Help

RITCHIE THREW HIS clothes on in fifteen seconds flat. In less than a minute the boys were rushing out of the front door.

The gale hit them like a wall. They staggered across the street and fought their way to the harbourside. There they stood teetering on the quay and clutching each other's arms.

"Ritchie!" Mark bawled over the din of the storm. "We're dreaming — we've got to be!"

"*No!*" Ritchie yelled back, shaking his head so his soaked hair flew. "We're not, we're *not!*"

He was all too hideously right. This was no dream! The lashing rain and the screaming wind were real — and so was the apparition coming towards them out of the roaring, howling night. It was crazy, it was impossible — but it was *happening!*

The lifeboat was halfway across the harbour. The grim, ghostly light still glared around her and even in the darkness Mark could see her clearly.

Her masts were broken and jagged and all that remained of the sails were a few tatters of canvas streaming like torn flags. Seaweed lay in tangled heaps on the deck. The hull was encrusted with barnacles — and beneath them, some faded letters were just visible.

The letters spelled out the name: *Charlotte Henty*.

Then Mark saw the men on board. And he felt as if his blood had turned to water in his veins.

The lifeboat crew were pale and deathly. Their old-fashioned oilskins streamed with water, and under their sou'westers their eyes were dead, black hollows in their skulls. An eerie light shone round them. They were not living men. They *couldn't* be.

They were staring fixedly at the boys, and Mark felt those stares piercing through him. Then one of the ghosts slowly raised a hand. The terrible figures shuffled aside — and Mark's pulse lurched as he saw what was behind them on the deck.

Five other men were sailing with the ghost crew. And they *were* alive. They were huddled together like terrified animals, their faces dead-white and their eyes glazed with shock. Their clothes and life jackets were instantly recognizable. Like the ghosts, they were lifeboatmen — but from the present and not the past.

Suddenly an awful, strangled moan broke from Ritchie's throat and above the noise of the storm Mark heard his voice go quavering up in a despairing cry.

"*Roy . . . Oh my God, ROY!*"

He lurched forward towards the edge of the harbour wall. "Ritchie, look out!" Mark yelled. He made a frantic grab for Ritchie's arm and hauled with all his strength. Ritchie teetered. They reeled together like crazy dancers as Mark struggled to drag his cousin back from the edge. Then their feet tangled; Ritchie tripped, stumbled, and the next instant they both fell to their knees.

Ritchie crouched on the quay, gasping and shuddering. His face was as white as the faces of the ghost crew and he looked as if he was going to be sick. Mark gripped his shoulders and forced himself to look at the spectral boat once more.

Roy's haggard face stared back across the water and the truth slammed home to Mark. The *Charlotte Henty*, lost over seventy years ago, had returned with her long-dead crew. And the men of the present-day lifeboat were sailing with them.

One of the ghost crewmen raised his hand again. Something about his face and black beard was familiar, but Mark was too dazed to think straight. Then the ghost's lips moved and a weird, echoing voice rang out from the tossing boat, reaching the boys even above the noise of the wind and sea.

"Rit-chie and Mark . . . Rit-chie and Mark . . ."

Ritchie's head jerked back and his mouth dropped open. And Mark's memory jolted back to the photo in the bar of the One and All. The black-bearded man was their great-granddad.

Ritchie's mouth worked violently and his teeth were chattering, but he couldn't make a sound.

"*Ritchie . . . Mark . . .*" The unearthly voice was flung ashore by the gale. "*You have to help us . . . Help us all . . .*"

"H-h-help . . .?" Ritchie found his voice at last, but it was no more than a whimper.

"*We failed to save the ship, and now we cannot save ourselves. Not until the old wrong is put right. Help us, Ritchie and Mark . . . Help us . . .*"

Ritchie's paralysis snapped and he screamed at the top of his voice; not to his great-granddad but to his brother.

"Roy!" His fists clenched, pounding the wind. "Roy, for God's sake, get ashore! Get away, jump, anything, just get *away* from there!"

But Roy shook his head wildly. Gripping the lifeboat's gunwale, he leaned forward and shouted back. "I can't! None of us can — we've got to stay!"

"No!" Ritchie yelled.

"Listen to me!" Roy begged distraughtly. "It was the song, Ritch, Trevorgie's song! It brought the past back to life! We've got to complete the circle — we've got to make amends for what Joe Trevorgie did!"

"*What?*" Ritchie cried. "I don't understand! Roy — *Roy!*"

The last word turned to a scream of

alarm, for as Roy's shout whipped past them and away on the wind, the spectral lifeboat began to move again. Slowly but surely, she turned right around. Then, without sails or oars or engine to power her, she headed away across the harbour.

Stunned and helpless, the boys watched her make way between the red and green lights at the harbour mouth. Then, as she reached the open sea, the shining light around her began to dim – and the boat and her crew faded away and vanished.

Mark stood rooted to the ground, staring at the spot where the phantom lifeboat had been. He wanted to run yelling for help, wake up the whole village, but he couldn't move a muscle.

Besides, who would believe this? He and Ritchie were the only ones who had seen the lifeboat.

He felt as if he was trapped in a monstrous nightmare. He didn't *believe* in ghosts! Yet tonight he had seen one. And something else, far worse than a ghost. Roy and the rest of the Polkerran crew . . . He had to help them! There was no choice for him. It was as if the ghost of Great-granddad had summoned him and Ritchie, and they had to answer the call. But how? They didn't even know whether Roy and the others were alive or dead.

Mark still stood rigid, feeling more frightened than he had ever been in his life. Then suddenly a scuff of feet jolted him back to his senses. Turning quickly, he was in time to see Ritchie start running along the quay.

"Ritchie!" Mark called. "What the heck are you doing?"

Ritchie ignored him. He was racing towards a ladder, set into the stone wall, that led down to the water. Mark shouted again but he still took no notice and with an awful feeling of foreboding, Mark took off after him.

Ritchie reached the ladder and plunged down it. Skidding to a halt at the top, Mark looked over the edge. Below him was a boat tied to a mooring ring by the ladder and rocking and bumping against rubber fenders on the choppy swell. She was a stubby-bowed little crabber, no more than seven metres long and with only a squat half-cabin for shelter. The name *Nimbus* was painted on her hull.

To Mark, she looked small and vulnerable, and his eyes widened in horror as he saw Ritchie swing from the ladder and jump on to the swaying deck.

"Ritchie, what the hell d'you think you're doing?" he bawled.

Holding on to the grab-handle beside the cabin, Ritchie turned and looked up at him.

"What does it look like?" His face was as white as Roy's had been, and grimly set. "I'm going after them. I'm going to save my brother! I've got to, Mark! Don't you see?"

The awful thing was, Mark *did* see.

The compulsion that drove Ritchie was driving him too. This was family and it was too strong to fight. But it clashed horribly with his fear, and he yelled, "Don't be a maniac — you can't just steal someone's boat and . . . and . . ." He waved a hand towards the harbour mouth. "And go out in *that*!"

"Can't I, then?" Ritchie snarled aggressively. "Watch me! Anyway, she's a mate of mine's boat. And you've got three seconds to decide whether you're coming!"

Mark's jaw dropped. "Whether *I'm* coming?"

"Yeah! 'Cause if you don't get aboard right *now*, I'm going on my own!"

Mark's mind was in chaos. This was totally crazy, he knew it, and every shred of sense in him was fighting against the craziness. But then Ritchie shouted again.

"You're in this as much as I am, Mark! They called both of us, remember? And we're the only ones who can do anything!"

Mark looked at the wild sea and his stomach turned over. He couldn't do this! He was too scared!

Then Great-granddad's words echoed in his mind. "*You have to help us . . . Help us all . . .*" It was like a command, and he couldn't resist. Whatever the danger, he couldn't let Ritchie go alone.

Without pausing to think, Mark scrabbled down the ladder. One foot groped in mid-air – then he clenched his teeth and jumped.

Chapter Five
Riding the Storm

"KEYS, KEYS . . ." RITCHIE scrabbled in the locker. "*Got 'em!*" He dived to the crabber's controls while Mark, clinging to the grab-handle, tried to make some sense of the confusion in his head. He felt sick and didn't know whether it was fear or seasickness, though they'd only been on board for a few seconds.

"OK, Ritch, calm, calm!" Muttering to himself, Ritchie slipped the key into the ignition then switched on the fuel. As the pump ticked, he flung a glance at Mark. "You OK?"

"Unh." Mark's reply could have meant anything, but Ritchie had already turned away. He fingered the throttle, checking it was in neutral, then pulled the starter. There was a vibration under Mark's feet, a strong whiff of diesel, and the *Nimbus*'s engine spluttered into life. For a few seconds it coughed and stuttered like something having a seizure, then it settled to an uneven, throaty burble.

Ritchie shouted jubilantly. "*Yeah!* Mark – cast us off astern!"

"Uh?" Mark didn't know what he was talking about.

"Astern, astern – the mooring – at the *back*, for crying out loud! Ohh –" Ritchie said a word that his parents didn't know he knew. He dived past Mark to do the job himself, then ran forward to cast off the bow rope.

Mark felt the boat start to swing outwards and shut his eyes as nausea surged in him. Then Ritchie was back. He nudged the throttle; the engine note steadied and strengthened and the crabber eased backwards, away from the quay wall.

As they started to move, Mark suddenly wanted to shout, "No, stop, let me off!" But his mouth and throat were so dry with fright that he couldn't manage so much as a croak. *I want out of this!* screamed a silent, panicking inner voice. But it was too late.

They were clear of the wall and the engine dropped briefly to tickover. Then Ritchie pushed the throttle forward, turned the wheel — and the burble swelled to a chattering roar that drowned the howl of the elements as the *Nimbus* swung away across the harbour.

Mark felt as if he had left his stomach behind on the quay wall. Everything around him was a blur of movement and noise: the engine's throbbing beat vibrating under him, the juddering impact of the swell, and the scream of the gale rising angrily as they headed towards open water.

Huddling at the entrance to the cramped half-cabin, he looked at the harbour and the village gliding past. There were no lights in any of the houses, but a thin bar of brightness showed under the closed door of the lifeboat house. People were awake in there, waiting and hoping for news. No one had seen the *Charlotte Henty*. No one knew what he and Ritchie were doing.

That thought terrified him and he grabbed his cousin's shoulder. "Ritch! We should have told someone!"

"Like who?" Ritchie retorted over the noise of the engine. "You think they'd've let us go?" He nudged the throttle another notch forward as if Mark's words were a challenge. The lights of the harbour mouth gleamed through the murk ahead. It made Mark realize that they themselves were unlit and he called, "What about our lights? Shouldn't we —?"

"All right, all right!" Ritchie altered course to clear the harbour wall, then flicked switches. Mark expected to see powerful beams stab the darkness like the headlights of a car. He was wrong. All that came on were the coloured navigation lights, a small white light at the top of the short mast, and another in the stern. Appalled, he yelled, "We can't see where we're going!"

"We're not supposed to!" Ritchie shouted back. "What do you think this is, the M1?" His hands tightened on the wheel. "Hang on to something — we're going to hit open water any minute, and then it'll get rough!"

Then it would get rough? Mark thought. Suddenly all the fears he had been trying to squash down overwhelmed him in a single, enormous surge. This wasn't just stupid — it was insane!

They were already pitching wildly, or so it seemed to him, yet they weren't even out of the harbour! The open sea was going to be a thousand times worse! And he didn't know the first thing about boats, and he hadn't got a life jacket, and he didn't want to *do* this! Something had forced him, some awful power from outside himself. He didn't want to give in to it. He was too frightened!

"Ritchie, turn back!" he pleaded.
"We can't do anything — we don't
know where the lifeboat's gone, we'll
never find it again! Oh Ritchie, *please!*
I'm scared!"

"Should have thought of that before,
shouldn't you? It's too late now, I'm not
going back for anyone!" Ritchie's head
flicked round and his eyes burned with
a ferocious emotion. "It's my brother
out there, Mark. It's Roy. You're not
going to do a Trevorgie on me — are
you?"

His words were like a smack in the
face to Mark. They hit him where it
hurt most — at the heart of his pride.
And that was enough for him. "I'm not
a coward!" he snapped furiously.

Ritchie glared back, and for an

instant Mark really believed that this was going to turn into a fight. But then Ritchie's expression changed. He grinned. It was right on the edge, but it *was* a grin.

"Who said you were?" he replied. "OK, then – here we go!"

Through the murk, the harbour lights glared like alien eyes. They came closer and closer, then in a blur they swept past to the right and left as the *Nimbus* sailed out between the protecting walls.

They met the open sea with a huge lurch that shook the boat from stem to stern. Ritchie yelled, "Hold ON!" and Mark clung to the grab-handle with all his strength. He had one glimpse of what looked like a grey-green wall hurtling towards him, and he shut his eyes in horror as the enormous swell tossed them like a cork in a flood. The harbour had been frightening enough – but this was a nightmare beyond anything he'd imagined!

"Mark!" Ritchie's voice reached him over the uproar of the wind and the sea and the *Nimbus*'s yammering engine. "Get right forward, like me! It's better!"

Hardly knowing what he was doing, Mark somehow made his feet move. Suddenly he was sheltered by the cabin's wooden walls and roof. They muffled the storm, if only a bit, and he found he could breathe again. Then Ritchie gave the engine a touch more throttle.

Its note strengthened to a snarl; they turned to starboard and their rolling motion became a switchback pitching as the crabber met the waves full on.

"Got to keep on this heading!" Ritchie said, holding grimly to the wheel. "That's the danger – getting broadside on. That's when you get swamped, or capsize."

"Thanks a bunch – I really wanted to know that!" Mark retorted through chattering teeth. His legs felt as if they had turned to jelly and his stomach was tied in so many knots that he couldn't even think about being sick. Some comfort! "Just keep telling me that you know what you're doing!" he added.

Ritchie laughed. "Course I do!"

"Where the hell are we going then?"

"Down coast, towards the Fowey estuary. From the course she was taking out of the harbour, I reckon that's the way the lifeboat went – and we're faster than she is!"

"But, Ritch –" Mark began.

Ritchie turned on him. "What?"

His eyes were dangerous, but Mark had to say it. "We don't even know that there *is* a lifeboat out here! It was a ghost, Ritch – *a ghost!*"

"And Roy was on board. He begged for our help!"

"Yeah, but –"

"Roy's not a ghost! He's alive, I *know* he is! And I'm going to find him!"

His mouth clamped shut and he turned his attention back to the wheel. Mark gave up. There was nothing else he could say. All he could do was hold on tight and pray that they would live to tell this story.

The *Nimbus* battled on, while Mark fought his own battle against panicking terror. The gale was tearing the clouds apart now so that bursts of moonlight broke through the tatters as though some storm giant was out there flashing a vast torch. The light-flashes were even more horrific than the darkness, for they showed the wild scene all too clearly. Heaving swell, churning wave-tops, flying spray . . .

Ritchie was struggling to keep the boat on course and Mark was certain that each towering wave would overturn them. But they kept going. One hour, two – Mark saw the time creeping by on his watch but it didn't mean anything. He felt they had been battering on for ever and would go on for ever. Until, suddenly, the engine began to sputter.

Ritchie swore and worked the throttle. For a few seconds the engine ran smoothly. Then it sputtered again.

Mark's head snapped round and when he saw his cousin's face his skin turned clammy. "What is it? What's wrong?"

Ritchie didn't answer but worked the throttle again, savagely this time. "Oh, no!" he hissed. "It can't, it *can't* −"

"Can't *what*?" Mark yelled.

Ritchie opened his mouth − and with a final gasp, the engine cut out.

"*Ritchie!*" Mark screamed. "*Get it started again!*"

Ritchie looked at him. All traces of colour had drained from his face and realization hit Mark as though someone had punched him. Ritchie was as terrified as he was. And with good reason.

"I can't start her again!" he moaned. "I didn't check. I didn't even *think* . . . The tank's empty, Mark. We're out of fuel!"

Chapter Six
Breakdown

"COME ON, MARK, come on! I can't do it all on my own – you've got to help me or we won't get out of this alive!"

Ritchie's frenzied plea broke through to Mark's petrified mind. And suddenly – though he'd never know how he did it – the will to survive overcame his terror. The world snapped back into focus, breath came in a rush and he cried, "What can I do?"

"We've got to keep her heading into the wind!" Ritchie shouted. "Need the sea anchor, to stop us broaching to!"

Mark hadn't the faintest idea what he meant but before he could ask, Ritchie added, "I'll get it – you come here, quick, and take the wheel."

"But I can't steer a boat!" Mark protested.

"You don't have to! Look, take hold. Now, just turn the wheel hard a-port, far as you can, and keep it there!"

He shoved Mark's hands on to the wheel, then lunged towards the locker. Mark swung the wheel as far as he could to the left (oh God, *was* that port? He hoped so!) while Ritchie scrabbled in the locker's depths.

"Anchor's – jammed!" he called, wrestling with it.

Mark turned. "Shall I –"

"*No!* Don't let go of that wheel!" Suddenly the sea anchor came free. The jolt smacked Ritchie's hand against the locker door and took the skin off his knuckles, but he didn't even notice. He scrambled round the side of the cabin and towards the bow, carrying the anchor. It looked to Mark like a big canvas bag attached to two ropes.

Mark watched as Ritchie threw the anchor overboard and paid out the ropes. The *Nimbus* was already beginning to veer from her heading, making the deck under his feet tilt and judder hazardously. The waves looked like avalanches toppling towards him.

Amid the racket of the storm, he could hear a new noise: an almighty crashing and banging that sounded as if it was coming from the engine compartment under the deck. But he couldn't worry about that. The engine was useless anyway; who cared if it tore itself to bits?

Ritchie came clambering back to the cabin. He was soaked with spray. "That'll help keep us straight," he said breathlessly. "Here, I'll lash the wheel now so you won't need to keep hanging on to it."

As he finished tying the lashing, a tremendous grinding noise came from below – and the sound of something falling heavily.

"What the —?" Ritchie spun round, and his eyes bulged with horror. "The lights — oh NO!"

He flung himself towards the engine compartment. Mark realized now that all four of the crabber's lights had gone out. He staggered after Ritchie and together they hauled up the engine cover. Ritchie had a torch in his pocket; he shone it down . . .

The crabber's battery lay on the compartment floor. It had broken from its mounting and the plastic case had split, spilling acid that hissed and steamed as it mingled with the water in the bilge. An acrid stench filled their nostrils and stung their eyes. Hastily, Ritchie slammed the cover shut again.

They stared at each other as the truth dawned. No engine, no radio — and now, no lights.

"Oh, my God, Ritchie . . ." said Mark. "What are we going to do?"

Ritchie scrambled up and floundered his way back to the cabin. "The sea anchor should let us hold our heading," he said breathlessly. "But without lights . . ." He swallowed. "The river estuary's somewhere ahead. Let's just hope there's no china-clay ships going in or out tonight. 'Cause if there are, they won't see us till it's too late!"

Mark shut his eyes at that thought. "There's got to be something we can do!" he said desperately. "Tie your torch to the mast or something —"

"No one'd see that till they were

almost on top of us!" Then Ritchie stiffened. "What the heck am I doing – there'll be flares, of course there will! Mark, quick, look in the locker!"

Mark dived, rummaged and found what looked like several Roman candles. "These?"

Ritchie spared a rapid glance. "That's them! There's a cord. You have to hold the flare at arm's length and pull the cord. *Hurry!*"

Mark tried to take in the shouted instructions. But he had never seen a flare before let alone handled one, and everything went wrong. He couldn't find the cord in the dark, then didn't know which way to pull it, and he fumbled awkwardly while Ritchie got more and more impatient.

"Come on, come *on*! It's not that difficult!"

"I can't!" Mark wanted to hurl the whole lot overboard, he was so frustrated. And Ritchie's shouting only made him clumsier.

Suddenly, in a bigger break in the clouds, the moon appeared. The sea lit up in a heaving mass of black and silver, and away to their right, Mark saw the ominous dark bulk of the coastline.

And something else.

"Ritchie!" he yelled, frantically pointing. "What's that, over there?"

Ritchie craned to look and his eyes widened. "Rocks!" The black humps of them were all too visible now, fringed with white spume. His face haggard, Ritchie said, "I didn't think we could have come this far — the tide's driven us faster than I reckoned! They're . . . they're the rocks where the wreck happened, Mark. The wreck seventy years ago . . ."

Stunned, Mark stared. Then with a shock he realized that the rocks were slowly but surely getting nearer. The sea was driving them shorewards, forcing them towards that deadly menace.

"Ritchie, we're too close!" he shouted.

"You don't have to tell me!" There was stark dread in Ritchie's voice. "But we're stuck — we're being driven on to the lee shore! We're going to go on to the rocks!"

His last words struck horror through Mark. He didn't care about lee shores and other words that he didn't even understand properly. But rocks – he understood that all too well!

Then suddenly something huge and dark, that was not the sea and not the rocks, loomed out of the wild night ahead of them. Lights glared through the murk – red, green, white – and the shapeless bulk suddenly resolved into the towering hull of a ship.

Ritchie gave an incoherent yell as he saw it. Mark's mouth opened too – but his own cry jammed in his throat. His mind raced back to the story of the wreck of seventy years ago. And he remembered the phantom lifeboat and her crew.

"It's a ghost . . ." He heard his own quavering voice as if from a million miles away. "Ritchie . . . it's the ghost of the cargo ship!"

For a single moment, Ritchie almost believed it. But only for a single moment, before the truth slammed into his brain.

"That's no ghost!" he screamed. "It's as real as we are — and it's heading straight for us!"

Chapter Seven
Man Overboard!

"GIVE ME THAT!" Ritchie whirled round, snatched the flare from Mark's hand and fired it skywards. Mark saw the brilliant light sear up into the night. It hung above the crabber for a moment, then the gale caught it and it was whisked away downwind.

Ritchie fired a second flare. The *Nimbus* was rolling horrifyingly now. Then suddenly, like the voice of some nightmare monster, the eerie howl of the cargo ship's horn boomed out above the noise of the wind and sea.

"They've seen us!" Frantically, Ritchie started to flash his torch, signalling SOS in Morse code. Three short, three long, three short —

"It's no use, Ritch!" Mark yelled. "They're coming straight at us! They'll never stop in time!"

The ship was changing course, veering to starboard. But it was far too late. The crabber was right in the huge vessel's path — there was nothing anyone could do to avoid a collision!

The ship bore down on them like a

vast, toppling wall, and the last of Mark's self-control exploded into uncontrollable terror. He shut his eyes and screamed – there was nothing else he could do – and through the panic in his mind he heard Ritchie screaming too.

They were going to be run down! They were going to be smashed to splinters by the relentless bulk surging towards them! They were going to drown, they were going to die –

But then he realized that Ritchie wasn't just screaming. He was bawling his name: "*Mark! MARK!*"

Mark's eyes snapped open. And bulged in their sockets.

Out of a trough between two towering swells, a third boat had appeared. It had masts and sails, and men in oilskins were hunched at a bank of oars. It was the *Charlotte Henty* – the old lifeboat! Mark's mind reeled with disbelief. And on the heels of his shock came a stunning surge of hope.

"Ritchie! Mark!" A voice roared out across the water and the boys saw their great-granddad. He was standing up and swinging a weighted rope; he cast it towards the crabber. "Catch hold, boys!"

Ritchie lunged. The thought flashed through Mark's mind: *the rope can't be real, not if the boat's a ghost!* But it was real. It smacked into Ritchie's hands and Great-granddad shouted, "Heave on it, boy, till you get the warp!"

Ritchie pulled with all his strength.

The heaving line came in, and attached to it was a stronger warp line. Ritchie made it fast to the *Nimbus*'s bow and the lifeboat went about, taking them in tow.

Great-granddad shouted encouragement to his crew. With the men rowing powerfully, the *Charlotte Henty* cut across the cargo ship's path. The crabber lurched and pitched after it and Mark saw the ship's immense hull cleaving through the sea, seemingly almost on top of them. He screamed again, certain they would be run down – but at the last moment both the lifeboat and the *Nimbus* pulled clear.

With hardly anything to spare, the moving mountain of the cargo ship swept past. Men were at the rail, shouting and waving agitatedly, and the horn boomed out again.

"Look out for the wash!" Ritchie cried to Mark. His warning came too late. The crabber was bucking like a mad horse, and Mark felt the deck heave under him as the ship's wash hit them. He staggered, hands clawing despairingly for the grab-handle. But his fingers closed on empty air, and in a flailing windmill of arms and legs he reeled across the deck. The world turned upside down – and he pitched over the crabber's side.

Churning water rose to meet him and Mark plunged into its ice-cold fury. Salt water filled his mouth and nose. There was a roaring in his ears, and his eyes were blinded. He thrashed in wild panic. Then the sea flung him upwards again and he broke surface with a choking gasp that turned to a scream. "*Help! Help me!*"

Mark was a good swimmer. At school, he was one of the best. But a sports-centre pool was a world away from the deadly power of a storming sea. He had no life jacket and his sodden clothes were hampering him. Struggling, panicking, he felt as if a whole world of water was seething and crashing in on him.

He could dimly hear voices shouting, and through streaming eyes he glimpsed the lifeboat tossing on the waves. The crew were trying to reach him but they couldn't get close enough. And the sea was dragging

Mark down. It was too strong. He couldn't fight it. He was going under . . . he was going to drown . . .

Then with a blur of movement, a figure jumped over the lifeboat's side. Arms thrashing, he swam towards Mark, calling, "Hold on, lad, hold ON!" But Mark couldn't keep his head above the surface any longer. He was swallowing water, slipping under and there was nothing he could do to save himself.

Strong hands grabbed him as he slid into churning darkness. He felt them lock under his arms, felt a giddying rush, and came up spluttering and gagging. For a shocked instant he saw the face of the lifeboatman who had rescued him. His hair was plastered wet to his skull but its colour was unmistakable. Blond. So blond it was almost white.

"Joe . . . Trevorgie . . ." Mark croaked.

"All right, all right!" yelled a voice in his ear. "I've got you! Don't struggle! Lie on your back and try to keep still. Trust me – I'll get you out of this!"

There was a line clipped to Trevorgie's jacket, stretching back to the lifeboat. A swell lifted them like corks and, as they rose, Mark saw the boat again.

It had changed! The masts and sails were gone and so were the men at the oars. In their place was a streamlined hull, high cockpit, radio aerials, radar – the *Charlotte Henty* had vanished back into history. And the present–day boat, which everyone had feared lost with all hands, had returned!

Hooded figures were hauling the line in now. Slowly but surely, Mark and his rescuer were towed to safety. Hands reached down to them, pulling Mark up out of the sea. He collapsed on the lifeboat's deck and a blanket was wrapped round him as the crewman was also heaved aboard. Shivering with cold and shock, Mark turned his head to look at the man who had saved his life.

A familiar face gazed back at him and the crewman managed a shaky grin.

"Lucky for you we were around, eh, Mark?" said his cousin Roy.

Chapter Eight
Cold Light of Dawn

ROY CAME DOWN the companionway
and said, "We're in sight of the harbour
lights now. Home soon. And then you
two'll get the rollocking you deserve!"

Mark and Ritchie exchanged a look.
They had changed their sodden clothes
for sweaters and blankets and had been

given hot chocolate drinks. Then they sat together in the small below-decks cabin while the lifeboat headed home. They couldn't see the outside world but a while ago Roy had told them that conditions were improving. The gale had started to die down, though the sea was still tremendous. On the eastern horizon the first cold light of dawn was showing.

Mark's head was full of confused feelings. Fright and shame and relief – and, more than anything, gratitude to the men who had saved him and Ritchie. He could hardly believe that he was alive. He could hardly believe that tonight had happened. But the proof was coming home with them: the *Nimbus*, in tow, with a lifeboat crewman on board. Oh yes, it had been real. All of it. And that left him with a whole lot of unanswered questions.

Where had the lifeboat — the present-day lifeboat — *been* for the past two nights? None of the crew had said a word about that, not even Roy. And though Mark wanted to ask, he couldn't summon up the nerve.

He told himself that the men were too busy concentrating on getting home to be bothered with questions. But, truthfully, he hadn't asked because part of him was scared to hear the answer. Something very, very weird had happened to the Polkerran lifeboat. Or rather, life*boats*.

For Mark and Ritchie hadn't dreamed any of this. The old *Charlotte*

Henty, lost over seventy years ago, *had* come back. And so had her long-dead crew. Mark knew who had saved him from drowning. He'd *never* forget that face and hair.

A little while later, Roy came down again and said that they had reached the harbour. Wrapped in their blankets, Mark and Ritchie shuffled up on deck. In the growing light they could see a crowd of people on the quay. News had been radioed ahead and it looked as if the whole village had turned out to welcome their lifeboat back.

Remembering what Roy had said, Mark dreaded the reception he and Ritchie would get. But Roy was looking at him again and suddenly he winked.

"Don't worry, Mark," he said.

"They'll be too glad to see us, and too busy making sure we're all in one piece, to be too rough on you!"

Roy didn't seem the least bit angry with them, Mark thought. In fact, none of the lifeboatmen did, and that was strange. He wanted to talk to Ritchie about that but had been too afraid of being overheard. It was another mystery that would have to wait.

Over the noise of the sea and the lifeboat's engines, they couldn't hear the shouting from the quay as they sailed in. But they could see the excitement. People were waving, signalling, punching fists in the air. Uncle Chris and Aunt Jen were at the front of the crowd. Aunt Jen was crying and so were quite a few others.

An ambulance and two police cars were waiting on the hard, and Mark's heart sank. There'd be official trouble to face as well. Stealing the crabber would only be the start. They must have broken just about every rule of the sea there was.

He glanced at Ritchie. He'd seen the ominous signs too but he only shrugged helplessly.

"Can't be helped, can it?" he said. "We can't turn back time –"

He stopped as he realized what he'd said and they stared at each other for a moment. Roy, who had heard them, frowned. He seemed about to say something. But then he changed his mind and looked quickly away.

The lifeboat nosed into the stone

steps at one end of the quay. The engine noise sank to an idling burble and the sudden relative quiet jolted Mark back into the real world. There were people everywhere, jostling on the harbour. Hands helped him and Ritchie to their feet and hurried them up the steps. Suddenly they were in the middle of a crowd.

Everyone seemed to be talking at once: some laughing, some angry, all firing questions. Mark's brain whirled helplessly. Then figures in dark-blue uniforms surrounded them, and Uncle Chris was there, not knowing whether to hug Ritchie or shake the life out of him and trying to do both.

Mark heard Ritchie protesting that they didn't want doctors or ambulances or any of that rubbish, and Mark joined in: "I'm OK, I'm fine, honest, I don't need to go to hospital."

Maybe, he thought later, people were made of sterner stuff round here, for to his enormous relief they listened. Within minutes the boys were inside the One and All with a brisk but friendly doctor from the local practice.

Mark's last clear memory that morning was of the doctor saying, "They're both fine – nothing that a day or so's rest won't fix. Lucky it isn't winter or we'd have had a couple of cases of hypothermia to deal with. Mark's a bit shocked, though. I'll give him something for that . . ."

Mark was told to drink something that the doctor put into his hands. He quickly began to feel drowsy and minutes later, with the background hubbub of voices in his ears, he fell soundly, blissfully asleep.

"Mark?" The voice hissed outside his bedroom door. "Mark! You awake?"

Mark struggled upright, wondering what on earth he was doing in bed in broad daylight. "Yeah . . . yeah, I'm awake."

Ritchie came in and as he shut the door Mark's memory came to life. "Ritch! What time is it?"

"Just gone three."

Astonished, Mark pushed the duvet back. Someone had put him in his pyjamas. He started to rummage in the chest of drawers for some clothes.

"Are you OK?" Ritchie asked.

"I'm fine. Just hungry. What's been happening?"

Ritchie rolled his eyes. "Don't ask! I've had it in the neck from the coppers, the coastguards, then Dad, and then Mum all over again when he'd finished! Oh yeah, and from Dave Lewarne. Nearly forgot him. He's the guy who owns the *Nimbus*." He grimaced, then his face relaxed. "Could've been worse, though. Everyone's so glad to see the lifeboat back safe, they're going a bit easy on us."

"Like Roy said," Mark commented.

"Yeah. Talking of Roy . . . he wants a word with us. Privately, he said."

Mark's pulse quickened. "Privately?"

They were both thinking the same thing. Ritchie nodded and Mark said, "When?"

"The guys from the coastguard and air-sea rescue have finished getting the cox's report, and they've cleared the crew to talk to the press," Ritchie said. "There are a couple of reporters downstairs now waiting to see them. Roy says to go in with them and hear the story."

"Right." Mark shoved his feet into his spare trainers. "The press don't want to talk to us, do they?"

"Dunno. Probably." Then Ritchie paused. "Mark, look . . . if they do, then I don't think we should tell them what *really* happened. You know?"

Mark looked at him levelly. "You

mean . . . about the *Charlotte Henty*."

It was the first time anything had actually been said aloud about it. Ritchie nodded. "Yeah. About that. If they ask . . . it was our lifeboat that came. And it was Roy who jumped in after you."

A prickling sensation ran down Mark's spine. So Ritchie had seen that. He, too, had recognized Joe Trevorgie.

"Right," he agreed in a small, taut voice.

There was no need to say any more.

Chapter Nine
Secrets

WHEN HE WALKED into the bar down-stairs, Mark suddenly knew what it must feel like to be a rare animal in a zoo. Ritchie's "couple" of reporters was more like eight or nine, including some from the local radio station.

And there were photographers. They

had the crew posing in front of the old lifeboat photos on the wall, and Mark and Ritchie had to be in the shots too. Then they wanted a picture of Mark shaking hands with Roy, then another of Mark and Ritchie together. Finally, though, they finished. Now, it was the reporters' turn.

At last, Mark and Ritchie heard what had really happened to the lifeboat.

Like the others who had answered the distress call, the Polkerran crew had failed to find any sign of a ship. But when they tried to call back to shore, they found their radio was completely dead. The coxswain gave orders to turn for home. Then, on the way back, the engines started playing up.

"Right old do, that was," the oldest

crewman said. "What with that and our communications out, we were proper b–"

"All right, Bev! You turned the air blue then, no need to do it again!" the cox interrupted hastily. "Anyway, we didn't know what was wrong. We started back, then suddenly all our navigation equipment went on the blink too. Compass, radar, everything – it just went haywire.

"Then to top it all, we ran into some freak weather condition. That's what it must've been, we reckon, though none of us had ever seen anything like it before."

"What *was* it like?" a reporter asked.

"Well . . ." The cox frowned uneasily. "It's hard to say. Everything around us went . . . dark."

"Like we were in a fog," another man agreed. "Only there wasn't any fog, of course. But we just couldn't see where we were going."

The darkness, they thought, could only have lasted a few minutes. When it cleared, they were astonished to find themselves in the calmer waters of a cove. Without the compass, they must have gone off course and sailed in to shore.

"There were rocks in the cove, so to get out safely we'd have had to go astern and back out," the cox said. "But she wouldn't. The engines were really playing up by then and we couldn't get her to respond properly. So I decided the safest thing to do was beach her in the cove and see if we could fix the problem."

And that was where the strangest thing of all had happened. The tide was ebbing but there was enough water left for them to run the lifeboat on to the beach. The anchor was pitched in the shingle and more lines fixed among the rocks to hold the boat securely. The crew climbed back on board to start checking the engines and systems. And every single one of them fell sound asleep.

One instant they were wide awake, getting on with the job in hand. The next . . . "Well, if I live to be a hundred I won't ever be able to explain it," said the cox. "But we all went spark out. Didn't know about anything till we woke up again, all at the same moment."

"How long did you sleep for?" asked the reporter.

"It was still dark. But when I looked at my watch — it's a twenty-four-hour one and it's got the date on too — I realized that we'd slept the clock nearly right round."

"Twenty-two hours, to be exact," said another crewman.

Several of the pressmen whistled astonishment. Mark and Ritchie eyed each other, and Mark's spine tingled once more.

"Thing was," the cox continued, "the engines were working again. Perfect. She started up sweet as you like. The radio was still out, but the navigation systems were fine. So", he shrugged, "seemed the best thing to do was get under way again before anything else happened."

"Or before we had any more dreams," a man behind him muttered.

The reporters didn't hear that. But Mark and Ritchie did, and so did Roy. He shot the man a glare and one hand moved, warning him to keep quiet.

Heading for Polkerran, with the engines now running smoothly, the lifeboatmen had seen the lights of the cargo ship and were keeping a safe distance when Ritchie's distress flares went up. It was sheer chance, the cox said – and nothing short of a miracle – that they were there.

Everyone knew the rest of the story, he added modestly, so there wasn't much point going over it all again.

They rescued the drifting crabber, and boats and crews got back in one piece. Oh, and just before they saw the boys, the radio started working again. No idea why. It just did.

"Fate was on your side, wouldn't you say?" asked one of the reporters.

The cox thought about the question for a few moments.

"*Something* was," he said at last. "I reckon we'd all agree on that. *Something* was."

The reporters wanted to interview Mark and Ritchie. But to their relief, Aunt Jen stepped in. The boys had had enough for one day, she said firmly. If they were going to talk to the press at all, they could do it tomorrow. Mark uncrossed his fingers when he heard this. There was no way he dared say anything to anyone until he'd had a chance to talk properly to Ritchie.

And to Roy.

No one had eaten yet, and in all the chaos there was no chance of sitting down to a proper meal. But when the press people finally left, Aunt Jen told Roy and the boys to grab something before anyone else came to interrupt them. It was the chance they had been looking for. They microwaved two pasties and a steak-and-onion pie from the pub's supplies, and escaped to the privacy of Mark's room.

Ritchie, going in last, shut the door and leaned against it. "OK," he said uneasily. "So who's going to start?"

Roy bit into his pasty. "It's not who, is it? It's where."

"Downstairs", Mark said, "one of the crew said something about dreams."

Roy gave him a sharp look. "So you heard that, did you? OK then. I'll tell you. But you've both got to swear that you'll never, *ever* mention it to anyone else, and especially not anyone from the crew. Right?"

"Right," Ritchie and Mark agreed.

So Roy told them. The rest of the crew would never talk about it, he said, not even among themselves. They were afraid people would laugh at them or think they were crazy. And they were right because, when they fell asleep so uncannily in the cove, they had all had exactly the same dream. A dream in which they were sailing in the lifeboat that had been lost all those years ago.

The old crew were there, Roy said. Great-granddad. Joe Trevorgie. All the men from the faded photo. And somehow – though they couldn't begin to explain it – the present-day crew knew that the spirits of those men were trapped in a kind of limbo.

Joe Trevorgie's cowardice had cost them their lives. And until he found a way to make amends, he and his companions would never truly be at rest.

"It all seemed so real in the dream," Roy said in a low, serious voice. "Spooky. Like we just *had* to believe it. And as for what happened afterwards, when we found you two . . ."

His voice tailed off. "You saw it, then," Ritchie said softly. "The *Charlotte Henty*. And Great-granddad . . ."

"Yes. We saw it." Roy paused. "Trevorgie jumped into the sea when I did. We both went after Mark. Got to him at the same time, and then . . . then Trevorgie and the old boat just . . . vanished."

Mark stared towards the window. The gale was blowing itself out now. The sea still looked dark and savage, but the sky showed patches of blue and the sun was breaking through. He thought of the old lifeboat, and of ghosts . . .

"They won't come back again," Ritchie said. "They don't need to, not any more."

Mark nodded. He understood now.

Thanks to Joe Trevorgie's bravery – and Roy's – the old wrong had been put right. The spirits of the lifeboat crew were at rest, and the curse Roy had awoken by singing Trevorgie's song was broken for good.

He looked at Roy and said, "We won't tell. Not anyone, not ever."

Roy smiled. "I know. A sort of pact, eh? Our secret."

They both glanced at Ritchie and, as if at some silent command, all three of them reached out and clasped hands.

"Yes," said Mark. "Our secret."

Chapter Ten
Headline News

THE ONE AND All was crowded that evening. Mark and Ritchie could hear the hum of voices in the bar downstairs as they sat in Ritchie's room. They were glad to be away from all the excitement, and didn't even feel like talking. In one way, there was so much to talk about that they didn't know where to begin. In another, there was absolutely nothing to say.

Mark was flicking through a magazine while Ritchie idly twiddled with the tuning on his radio. They had been listening to some music but the DJ changed and the next one played boring stuff, so Ritchie was looking for something better.

He tuned in to the local station. The news was on. Polkerran was the big headline of the day, but Ritchie didn't want to listen to that. He started to twiddle again – then suddenly stopped as he heard what the newscaster was saying.

". . . And there's a new twist tonight to our main story. An unidentified wreck was discovered yesterday in a cove down the coast from Polkerran Harbour. It was spotted by the crew of a search-and-rescue helicopter, and was feared at first to be the missing Polkerran lifeboat.

"The severe weather made a closer search impossible but today, with conditions improving, investigators have been able to reach the cove.

"The mystery wreck has now been identified as the *Charlotte Henty*, the Polkerran lifeboat which was lost with almost all her crew during a rescue operation seventy years ago. Coastguards say that . . ."

The newsreader's voice was blurred by the thick pounding of Mark's pulse in his ears. Slowly, nervously, he turned to look at Ritchie. Ritchie had heard. And his face had turned pale.

Suddenly Ritchie dived for the radio and turned up the volume.

". . . how the *Charlotte Henty* could have been washed ashore, nearly intact, after so many years is a question that perhaps will never be answered," the newsreader was saying. "The hull will now be brought back to Polkerran and it is hoped that she will be restored and displayed as a memorial to the men who died in that long-ago disaster . . ."

"Switch it off," Mark said quietly.

Ritchie did. Silence fell in the room. Then at last Ritchie spoke.

"A question that perhaps will never be answered . . ." He mimicked the newsreader's tone, but his face was deadly serious.

"*We* could answer it," whispered Mark.

"Yeah. Us, and Roy, and the crew."

"But we won't."

Ritchie nodded agreement. But he didn't say another word. There was no need to.

Not ever.